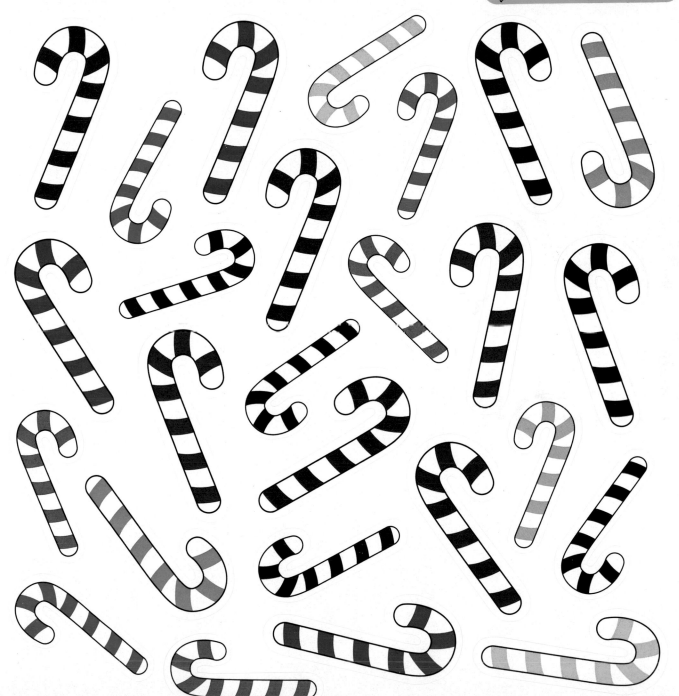

ISBN: 3-1A3-121193-1   © Scholastic Inc.

The Biggest Christmas Tree Ever

The Biggest Christmas Tree Ever

by Steven Kroll

illustrated by Jeni Bassett

Cartwheel
B·O·O·K·S ®

SCHOLASTIC INC.

New York   Toronto   London   Auckland   Sydney   Mexico City   New Delhi   Hong Kong   Buenos Aires

For Kathleen
— S.K.

For Ralph
— J.B.

Text copyright © 2009 by Steven Kroll.
Illustrations copyright © 2009 by Jeni Bassett.
All rights reserved. Published by Scholastic Inc.
SCHOLASTIC, CARTWHEEL BOOKS, and associated logos are trademarks and/or registered trademarks of Scholastic Inc.

Library of Congress Cataloging-in-Publication Data

Kroll, Steven.
The biggest Christmas tree ever / by Steven Kroll ; illustrated by Jeni Bassett. — 1st ed.   p. cm.
Summary: Clayton and Desmond learn that by working together, they can find the biggest Christmas tree ever.
ISBN-13: 978-0-545-12119-4 (pbk. : alk. paper)
ISBN-10: 0-545-12119-1 (pbk.)
[1. Mice—Fiction. 2. Christmas trees—Fiction. 3.Cooperativeness—Fiction.] I. Bassett, Jeni, ill. II. Title.

PZ7.K9225Bjn 2009   [E]—dc22   2008032874

ISBN-13: 978-0-545-12119-4
ISBN-10: 0-545-12119-1

20 19 18 17   40   18/0
Designed by Angela Jun
Printed in the U.S.A
First edition, September 2009

Once there were two mice who fell in love with the same
Christmas tree, but you had to see it to believe it.

Everyone in Mouseville loved Christmas trees. Every Christmas,
families all over town put up the biggest, most beautiful tree they could find.

But first came Thanksgiving. The day before the celebration, Clayton, the house mouse, took a walk around Mouseville. He knew he should be thinking about giving thanks, but the chill in the air reminded him of Christmas.

"You know what?" he said out loud. "This year I'm going to find the biggest Christmas tree ever!"

Not far away, Clayton's friend Desmond, the field mouse, said exactly the same thing.

That night, Clayton helped his mom and dad, his brother, Andy, and his sister, Trudy, make a special cheese casserole and a nut pie for Thanksgiving dinner.

Over at Desmond's house, Desmond and his brother, Morris, helped Uncle Vernon fix a big pot of vegetable stew and a cheesecake.

Everyone ate much too much. After dinner, Clayton's grandma and grandpa sat in the living room, holding their tummies and grumbling.

Over at Desmond's, the cousins from across the road stretched out on Uncle Vernon's sofa and took a nap.

The following morning, Clayton woke up early. He wanted to be first at Clara's Christmas Tree Farm at the edge of town. That way, he could have his pick of the biggest trees!

Over at Desmond's house, Desmond tumbled out of bed with the same thought.

Clayton hurried over to Clara's, but it was hard to go very fast. He was still too full of Thanksgiving dinner. By the time he reached the Christmas tree farm, he was out of breath. He looked around. No one else was there.

Moments later, Desmond arrived. He too was full of Thanksgiving dinner. He too had found it hard to hurry. He took a deep breath and stumbled inside.

Clayton wobbled down the rows of trees. Here was a nice one, but it was much too small. There was another, but it was squat and had a crooked top. Over there was a third, but it was average height and had big gaps between the branches.

Struggling down another row, Desmond was having the same problems.

Clayton leaned against a tree. It was scrawny and not very tall.
"I'll never find the tree I want," he said. "I'd better go home."

And not far away, squinting at another tree, Desmond said,
"I'll never find the tree I want. I'd better go home."

When Clayton reached his house, it was only the middle of
the morning. But he was still full, and he was tired. He fell back
into bed.

When Desmond reached *his* house, he too went back to bed.

Clayton woke up for lunch and spoke to his dad.

Dad said, "Go out this afternoon. Walk to the far edge of the Christmas tree farm. The biggest trees are there."

When Desmond woke up for lunch, Uncle Vernon told him the same thing.

That afternoon, Clayton went out again. At the very same time, Desmond did too.

Clayton walked to the far edge of the Christmas tree farm. He looked at one big tree after another, but none of them looked like the biggest Christmas tree ever.

Down another path, Desmond was having the same bad luck.

Starting to lose hope, Clayton peered around a very thick
trunk. Desmond peered around the same thick trunk. They bumped
heads and fell down.

"I bet *you're* looking for the biggest Christmas tree ever!"
said Clayton.

"I bet *you're* looking for the biggest Christmas tree ever!"
said Desmond.

"Why don't we find it together?" said Clayton.

"No one said we couldn't," said Desmond.

They set out through the rows of trees. They looked and looked until it was almost dark.

Just as they were ready to give up, there it was: a Christmas tree so big and so tall, it reached the sky!

"How will we cut it down?" Clayton asked. "It's much too big for the two of us."

"Where will we put it?" Desmond added. "It won't fit in your house or mine."

Clayton and Desmond smiled.

"Our families will help us," they said together.

And that is what happened. Clayton's dad and Uncle Vernon came out with their axes, and with the help of Clayton and Desmond, they chopped down the giant tree.

Both families called on friends and relations, and together they loaded the tree onto a hundred red wagons and pulled it to Clayton's front yard. There they decorated it with the most wondrous ornaments and colored lights . . .

. . . and on Christmas Eve, with all of Mouseville celebrating around it, the biggest Christmas tree ever lit up the entire hillside.

Clayton and Desmond shared a high five.

"We did it!" said Clayton.

"All of us together!" said Desmond.

Underwater Explorers

by Laura Johnson

PEARSON
Scott
Foresman

DK

What You Already Know

The hydrosphere is all of the water on Earth. It covers about 75 percent of Earth's surface. About 97 percent of the hydrosphere is ocean water, which has high salinity. There is very little fresh water on our planet, and about 70 percent of it is in the form of ice.

Most of our fresh water begins as rain or snow. The rain or melted snow that soaks into the ground is called groundwater. The layer of rock and soil that groundwater flows through is an aquifer. The top of the groundwater in an aquifer is called the water table. During periods of heavy rain, the water table rises. During drought, the water table falls. We need to use groundwater wisely or aquifers may become dry.

Surface waters include rivers, streams, and lakes. These are formed naturally from melting snow, rain, and groundwater. Reservoirs are lakes that form behind dams.

Some towns get their water from groundwater. Others get it from surface water that must be treated before it is safe to use. Chemicals and filters are used in the treatment process.

Water is always moving as it changes from one form to another. The repeated movement of water through the environment is called the water cycle. The steps of the water cycle include evaporation, condensation, and precipitation. Evaporation is the changing of liquid water into water vapor. In condensation, the water vapor turns into liquid. In precipitation, the water falls as rain, snow, sleet, or hail. Then the precipitation evaporates and the cycle continues. Sublimation is a variation of the water cycle. This occurs when ice changes directly into water vapor without melting first.

Clouds are an important part of the water cycle because they bring rain and snow. They form when water vapor changes into tiny water droplets or ice crystals.

People have always been interested in the world beneath the water. But the underwater environment is very hard to explore. In this book, you will learn how humans have met the challenges of exploring the Earth's oceans.

Underwater Exploration

About 75 percent of Earth's surface is covered with water. However, we know more about outer space than we do about the world beneath the seas. The main reason underwater exploration is so difficult is that people can't breathe underwater. Another problem is the great pressure of the water deep in the ocean. Water is almost one thousand times heavier than air. At the bottom of the ocean, all the weight of the water above pushes down with enough force to crush a person!

Oceanography is the study of the oceans and the things that live in them. Scientists who study oceans are called oceanographers. Oceanographers use diving gear and special vehicles that allow them to explore beneath the surface of the sea—even at great depths. There is an amazing world to discover beneath the sea. There are undersea mountain ranges with peaks taller than any on land. And there are canyons deeper than the Grand Canyon! There are even superheated deep-sea fountains surrounded by strange creatures. Read on to learn more about how oceanographers have been able to explore these environments and the fascinating things they have discovered there.

Ocean Depths

To study the ocean more easily, oceanographers divide the ocean into three major layers, or zones. Some oceanographers call them the sunlit zone, the twilight zone, and the midnight zone. Differences in conditions such as temperature and amount of light determine the kinds of plants and animals that can be found in each zone.

The layer closest to the surface is the sunlit zone. Because sunlight reaches this layer, the water is warmest here and photosynthesis can take place. This zone is home to a wide variety of plants and animals. In fact, most marine creatures live here, including fish, sea turtles, seals, and jellyfish.

The middle layer of the ocean is often called the twilight zone because only a small amount of sunlight reaches this water. No plants and few animals are found here. The water temperature is much colder, and there is not enough sunlight for photosynthesis to occur. The creatures that do inhabit this zone have interesting features that help them adapt to the dark, cold environment. Some of the fish that live here can even light up parts of their bodies like fireflies!

The midnight zone is below the twilight zone. It is completely dark and very cold. Many fish that live here have big jaws to help them scoop up a scarce food supply. Others are scavengers, eating any dead food that drifts to the ocean floor.

This zone begins at the surface and extends down about 650 feet. The sunlight quickly decreases in this zone. The seafloor here is called the continental shelf.

sunlit zone

This zone extends from 650 feet down to about 3,300 feet. In this zone, the seafloor is a steep cliff called the continental slope.

twilight zone

This zone extends from about 3,300 feet down to the deepest point of the ocean floor—about 36,000 feet. Nearly 90 percent of the ocean is in this zone. The seafloor here includes hot-water vents and deep trenches.

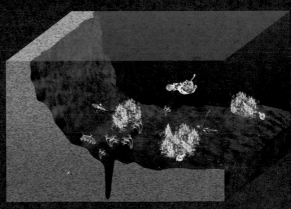

midnight zone

Scuba Diving

People have searched for ways to breathe underwater for thousands of years. Early divers breathed through hollow plant stems that stuck out above the surface of the water like modern-day snorkels. The ancient Greeks invented a special device called a diving bell. It was like a large, upside-down bucket pushed underwater to trap air. Divers could swim around and return to the diving bell when they ran out of air. Many years later, diving helmets were invented. Divers breathed air from hoses that ran between their helmets and the surface.

Today, scuba divers breathe air from tanks strapped to their backs. This air has been compressed, or squeezed under pressure, into a tank. This allows divers to carry a large amount of air in a small container.

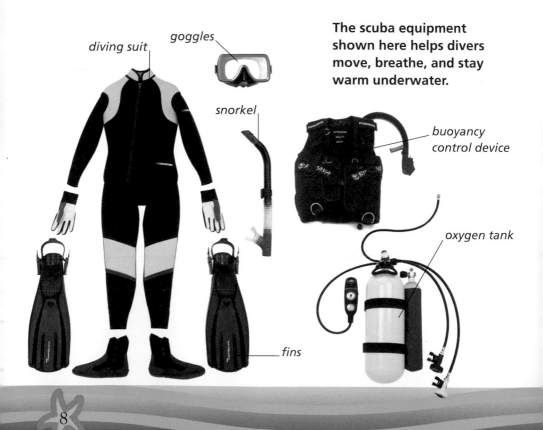

diving suit

goggles

snorkel

The scuba equipment shown here helps divers move, breathe, and stay warm underwater.

buoyancy control device

oxygen tank

fins

The compressed air flows through a hose from the tank to a regulator. The regulator lowers the pressure of the air, making it safe to breathe again. Scuba divers can safely descend about one hundred feet below the surface to explore the upper part of the sunlit zone.

The most dangerous part of scuba diving is not descending into the ocean but returning to the surface. Coming up too quickly after breathing pressurized air can cause gas bubbles to form in a person's bloodstream. This dangerous condition is called "the bends."

The term *scuba* is formed from the first letters in *s*elf-*c*ontained *u*nderwater *b*reathing *a*pparatus.

Submersibles and ROVs

To explore deeper ocean depths, scientists use underwater vehicles called submersibles and ROVs (remotely operated vehicles). A submersible is a small underwater vehicle that can safely carry people very deep in the ocean. It has a very hard shell that can stand the great pressure of the water. The crew is often made up of a pilot and one or two oceanographers. The oceanographers can conduct experiments, videotape the environment, and use a robotic arm to collect plant and animal samples. The crew can communicate with scientists on the surface ship.

One of the most famous submersibles is the *Alvin*, built by the United States in 1964. It is almost twenty-four feet long and can move about one-half mile in an hour. It can descend to a depth of about 14,800 feet.

The ROV *Jason Jr.* is used to explore shipwrecks at the bottom of the ocean.

ROVs are used to explore the deepest parts of the ocean. Instead of being operated by a crew, ROVs are connected by cable to a ship on the ocean's surface. An operator uses a joystick to control lights and video cameras on the ROV. The operator also controls claws that dig and collect samples from the ocean floor. Since no people are on board, ROVs can remain underwater for as long as the operator wants. They never have to come up for air, food, or water. They are also smaller than submersibles, so they can fit into tighter spaces.

The *Alvin* has made about four thousand successful research dives.

Mapping the Deep

Scientists use systems of sound waves to measure depth and map the uneven surface of the ocean floor. These systems are called sonar. Special instruments send out sound waves that travel from a ship to the ocean floor. When the sound waves hit the bottom, they bounce back to instruments on the ship. The instruments record the amount of time that passes between when the sound waves are sent and when they reach the ship again. By measuring how long it takes for the sound waves to return to the ship, the instruments can figure out how far away the seafloor is.

The colored bands at the bottom of the diagram show the different layers of sediment and rock that cover the ocean bottom.

undersea volcano

continental slope

abyssal plain

Then, computers use the echo readings to create maps of the seafloor. These maps include features such as mountains, ridges, volcanoes, or trenches. How accurate is this system? When mapping ocean features located three miles below the surface, the readings are off by only about six feet!

Most seafloor mapping is done with a special type of sonar that sends out multiple sound waves at the same time. This allows large areas of the sea to be mapped at once. However, there are still huge areas of the seafloor that have not been mapped.

mid-ocean spreading ridge

deep-sea trench

Mid-Ocean Ridges

The Earth's crust is made of huge plates, or sheets of rock. Underwater mountain chains, called ocean ridges, are found where some of these plates are separating. Ridges run through all the major oceans on Earth. In some places these ridges are a thousand miles wide and tower two miles above the seafloor. Even so, their peaks remain a mile or two below the surface of the water.

One of these ridges, called the Mid-Ocean Ridge, twists for 46,000 miles around the Earth. As in other ridges, a narrow canyon runs along the center of the Mid-Ocean Ridge. It is called a rift valley. These steep-sided valleys are places where the Earth's plates are being pulled apart.

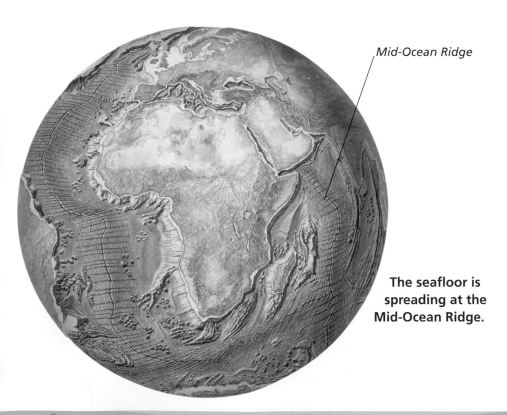

Mid-Ocean Ridge

The seafloor is spreading at the Mid-Ocean Ridge.

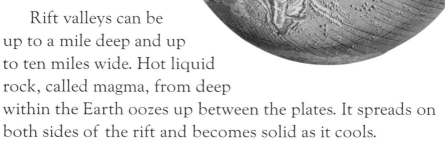

Undersea mountains dot the ocean floor but rarely rise above sea level.

Rift valleys can be up to a mile deep and up to ten miles wide. Hot liquid rock, called magma, from deep within the Earth oozes up between the plates. It spreads on both sides of the rift and becomes solid as it cools.

If you look at the map that shows the Mid-Ocean Ridge, you'll see that it looks like stitches on the seam of a baseball. The "stitches" are fracture lines along the rift valleys. These fractures, or breaks, occur as the ocean floor shifts and splits the mountaintops apart.

Seafloor Spreading

As magma is pushed up from deep within the Earth, it causes the seafloor to spread. But where can it expand to? The Earth's plates either slip under one another or try to slide past one another. This motion causes earthquakes and volcanoes.

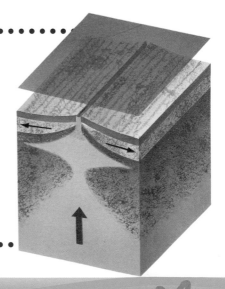

Smokers and Vents

In 1977 a crew onboard the *Alvin* was about eight thousand feet down in the Pacific Ocean when a thermometer alerted them to a sharp rise in temperature. Soon after that, the scientists saw a fountain of black water coming out of a crack in some rocks. Using a robotic arm, they moved a thermometer toward the black water. The thermometer melted! They were the first people to discover a hot water vent and a smoker.

Hot water vents form when cold ocean water seeps down through cracks in the seafloor and lands on hot rocks deep inside the Earth. There, the water heats up, sometimes to a temperature as hot as 750°F! Then it shoots back up through the Earth's crust. As the hot water travels through the rock, it dissolves minerals, such as iron, copper, and zinc, and carries them along.

When the water reaches the seafloor, a stream of hot water and minerals shoots out like a giant fountain. When the hot water meets the cold water of the ocean, the minerals harden into tiny crystals.

Crabs live near the vents and smokers on the seafloor.

The dark crystals make the fountains of water look like black smoke, so scientists call them black smokers. As the minerals sink back toward the seafloor, they form tubes that look like chimneys. These chimneys can quickly grow to be dozens of feet tall.

Surprisingly, many animals live near the vents and smokers. Many of these are tiny bacteria that make food from chemicals that spurt out of the vents. Other animals, such as worms, crabs, clams, and shrimp, feed on the bacteria. The bacteria allow these animals to live in an environment that could not normally support life.

Smoker chimneys can be black or white, depending on the color of the minerals they contain.

Mountains and Trenches

As you have learned, the Earth's crust is divided into huge sheets of rock called plates. Scientists believe there are about fifteen to twenty major plates that cover the Earth. These plates can move in three different ways. Sometimes they move away from each other. This movement causes seafloor spreading, as you learned earlier.

Sometimes plates move toward each other. If they collide, they can form mountains or trenches. When one plate slips below another plate, scientists call this subduction. This slipping action forms deep trenches. The deepest known trench is the Marianas Trench in the Pacific Ocean.

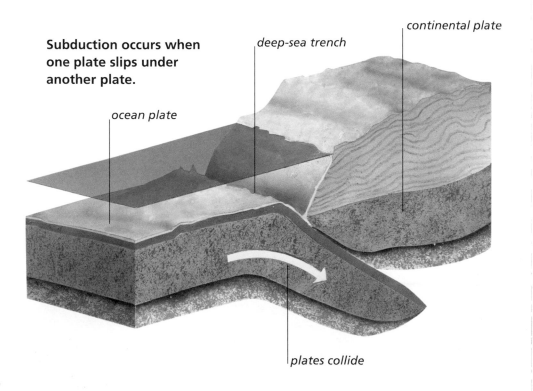

Subduction occurs when one plate slips under another plate.

deep-sea trench

continental plate

ocean plate

plates collide

If the plates crash and pile up on each other they can form mountains. These underwater mountains are called seamounts. Seamounts are hills and mountains that do not rise above the ocean's surface. Even though they do not break the surface of the

Each of the Hawaiian Islands is made up of the remains of at least one volcano. The island of Hawaii is made of five volcanoes.

water, some seamounts are thousands of feet tall. Plates can also slip past each other. There is no gap created between the plates and they do not crash. This type of plate action usually occurs in ocean basins, however it sometimes occurs on land. The San Andreas Fault in California rests on two plates that move in this way.

Voyage to the Bottom

In 1960, Jacques Piccard and Donald Walsh dove deeper than anyone else in history. They reached the bottom of the Marianas Trench in the Pacific Ocean, at a depth of 36,201 feet. They were in a bathyscaphe named the *Trieste I*. The word *bathyscaphe* means "deep boat."

Satellite Technology

Satellites have greatly changed the way scientists view and study the ocean. In the past, oceanographers had to gather data about ocean temperature, waves, and currents from ships. The information could only give them a "snapshot" of an area at the time it was studied. Soon after a ship left a location, conditions might have changed.

Using satellite technology, scientists are able to get a "big picture" of the world's oceans. This technology also supplies instant and constantly updated information about the seas.

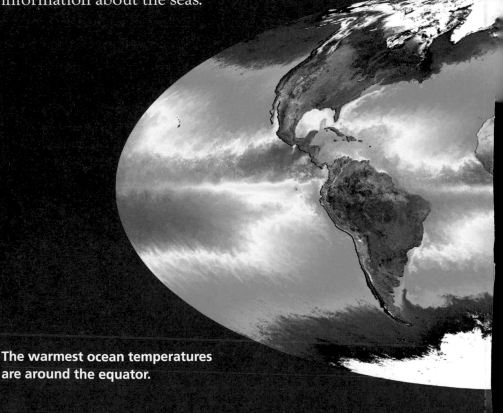

The warmest ocean temperatures are around the equator.

For example, heat-sensitive equipment gives information about the temperature of water at the sea's surface. In the map below, colors such as red, orange, and yellow represent warm temperatures. Greens, blues, and purples represent cooler temperatures. The same pictures can show water currents and the changes in water level.

Satellite images can also track pollution and show its sources. They can highlight areas that are rich in plant life, which provides food for marine animals. Satellites can be used to track animals such as sea turtles, whales, and fish. This kind of information helps scientists learn about the daily activities, habits, and migration patterns of these animals.

-2 5   10   15   20   25   30   35
degrees Celsius

Conclusion

Since ancient times, humans have wondered about what lies beneath the sea. But only recently has technology allowed us to travel safely under the water. Scuba diving equipment, submersibles, ROVs, sonar, and satellites are all useful tools for oceanographers. They have helped us learn many amazing things about the Earth's oceans.

Oceanographers divide the ocean into three major zones. Some oceanographers call these the sunlit zone, the twilight zone, and the midnight zone. Different kinds of life exist in each zone.

Scientists have discovered that the seafloor looks a lot like the land above sea level. Hills, valleys, mountain ranges, and trenches are created when the Earth's plates shift. These plates can move in three different ways. When they move away from each other, the seafloor spreads. When they move toward each other one of two things can happen. They may collide and form mountains, or one plate may slip below another creating a trench. The third way plates can move is parallel to each other. There are huge areas of the ocean floor yet to be explored. Who knows what discoveries will be made in your lifetime?

Glossary

crust   the outermost layer of the Earth

descend   to go from a higher place to a lower place

marine   having to do with the sea

oceanography   the study of the sea

seamount   mountain that does not rise above the ocean's surface

smoker   a fountain of water and dissolved minerals that shoots out of a vent on the seafloor

subduction   the action of one of Earth's plates slipping under another

trench   a deep groove in the ocean floor caused by one plate slipping under another